# Dangerous Potatoes

## Acknowledgements

To my wife Ann, thank you for saving my life.

My eldest daughter Lula, the original Monkeyman.

My boys and girls Jake, Callum, Olivia and Willow
for listening in wide eyed amazement.

My sister Jackie and my nephews Sean and Simon
for Easter egg hunts in Bluebell wood, (In the day time of course).

Mark, Joanne, Samuel and Toby for help with the finer details.

Special thanks to Roger King for pointing out my over use of the lowly comma
and Sarah Kershaw for relighting the fire

This book is born out of bedtime stories.

Never stop telling them.



Cover colouring and layout Steve Cripps

Editing and proof reading Mark Webb and Adrienne Staniford

Published by Diverze Publishing - www.diverze-publishing.com

First Edition - Printed 2012 in Great Britain by Diverze Print - www.diverze-print.com

# Foreword

Some children don't like soggy cabbage, smelly sprouts or bitter broccoli but, of course, everyone loves potatoes. They are just delicious chipped, roasted, mashed or fried. Unless, they happen to be Dangerous Potatoes! (Solanum Tuberosum Periculosum.)

"How can a potato be dangerous?" I hear you ask. Well, if you've never seen a Dangerous Potato you're very lucky. The children in this book weren't quite so lucky! But, you'll have to read the stories to find out just how dangerous potatoes can be!

Oh, but before you get started there's one more thing you need to know about Dangerous Potatoes. They can change nature around themselves. They can turn normal things into unusual things, because they are freaks of the vegetable world. And beware. Even listening to stories about Dangerous Potatoes can make strange things happen to you. However, the truth is, Dangerous Potatoes just want to be left alone and it's only when people bother them that problems begin. But isn't all of nature like that?!!!

The problems were only just about to begin for the children who lived in a strange sleepy little town, but for your own safety it's best you don't know where it is. No, I'm not going to tell you just incase you are tempted to go there and search for Dangerous Potatoes yourself. That would be asking for trouble. What I will say is it's a small picturesque little English town with wiggly, winding roads that amble between pretty, well-kept gardens. It's a bit of an old-fashioned place with lots of things left over from the olden days... Days which your mummy and daddy may remember. So if anything seems very old and strange in this book, just ask your parents.

Meanwhile here's a map of the town to get you started.

N
Timmy Trolley Bus' House
School
Bluebell Wood
Dangerous Potatoes
Beware.
Wiggley Windey Road
Monkeyman's Garage
Squinkle's house
Sweet shop
Wika Waka's house
Police Station. Jail

# Story Five

# squinkle

# Chapter 1

# Squinkle

'Squinkle' is a silly name, everyone knows that, and 'Squinkle' is an even sillier boy... Everyone knows that too, unless you're as silly as he is (which I seriously doubt). He doesn't know many things and he certainly can't blow bubbles or tie his shoelaces. If you asked him which way was 'up', he would have to lie down, because his brain would start to ache from such a difficult question. Poor Squinkle! He can't help it. He's just silly! He wears big thick glasses like magnifying glasses. In fact they actually might be magnifying glasses! He has black, flat, greasy hair with a center parting and a thin, white face. But there's something else you should know about him. He's the most loyal friend anyone could have.

Today, Squinkle was in the bathroom trying to clean his teeth, but he couldn't find the toothpaste because there was none! "I know," said Squinkle to himself. "I'll use some soap, I'm sure it will work just as well." Picking up a huge bar of soap in one hand and holding his toothbrush in the other, he started to rub the two together. But he soon got impatient with that and decided to rub the soap directly onto his teeth.

"I'll have the cleanest teeth in the whole wide world," he said to himself proudly as bubbles popped and foamed out of his mouth. "Who needs a toothbrush anyway? I bet Monkeyman wouldn't have thought of that." Feeling very pleased with himself, but with a funny taste in his mouth, he looked around for something else that would amuse him.

"Oooooh," he beamed, picking up his daddy's electric shaver. This is a bit naughty, which isn't like Squinkle. But he was probably being more silly than naughty.

"Mummy says I'm a big boy now, so maybe I should start shaving like daddy does?"

Looking at his reflection in the bathroom mirror he whizzed the buzzing shaver over his nose and under his chin, just like daddy did. He was having so much fun he started daydreaming and humming along with the sound of the shaver.

"Huuuuummmmmmmmmmm," he hummed, moving the shaver in wider and wider circles.

Unfortunately Squinkle was enjoying himself so much he didn't notice the huge clumps of hair falling to the bathroom floor. Finally though he stopped and looked at himself in the mirror.

"Yiiiiikkkkkkessss!" he screamed, his eyes bulging out of his head.

His scalp was almost bald except for a few forlorn tufts of hair left on the top. Even Squinkle realised he looked silly.

"Mummy will shout at me," he sniveled.

"And Timmy Trolley Bus will laugh at me," he cried.

"Everyone will laugh at me," he wailed.

Suddenly his eyes lit up.

"I know!" he said. "Daddy always splashes nice smelly stuff on after he shaves and I think it's to make his hair grow back. Maybe if I use enough it'll make my hair come back." He fumbled around for the aftershave and quickly found it. Eagerly he soaked his head and chin with the smelly liquid. For a second there was silence, as Squinkle looked for any signs of hair growth. Suddenly though, he let out a loud howl of surprise as it stung him. "Ow ow ow ow ow ow ow," he shrieked.

Then from downstairs he heard his mummy calling.

"Squinkle, what are you doing?" she shouted.
"Nothing mummy, just cleaning my teeth," he lied.
"Really well," he added hopefully.

Then he heard his mummy marching upstairs. Like a bald startled rabbit, he looked around desperately for a way to escape! He spotted the open bathroom window. As his mummy tried to open the door, Squinkle climbed out of the window and jumped into a nearby tree. Scrambling quickly down, he ran off to think about what to do.

# Chapter 2

# What to do?

Squinkle ran for what seemed like miles, muttering to himself, "What shall I do, what shall I do?" But suddenly he came across something very strange indeed. Standing before him was a tall plant, which seemed to be covered in hairy fluffy stuff. "What sort of tree is that?" he said to himself scratching his bald head. He thought for a moment and then said..... "Wow! It's a wig tree. That's just what I need, a wig."

So he grabbed a long stick and knocked one of the wigs down from a high branch and tried it on. It looked ridiculous. But he was so engrossed with his new look he didn't hear the little giggles and gurgles that came from behind 'the wig tree'.

"I wish I had a mirror," he said to himself. And then, as he turned round, he saw a mirror bush! "Wow, 'a mirror bush'. I've never seen one of those before either."

More giggling came from behind the 'mirror bush.' Then he turned to admire his reflection in one of the many different shaped mirrors that hung there. "Maybe I should try a different one," said Squinkle, adjusting the wig from side to side. After trying on quite a few wigs from the tree, he decided on a wig he liked. This one was so big the fringe kept getting in his eyes and he had to keep brushing it to one side with his hand.

"Mummy will never notice the difference now," he said as he looked at his reflection.

"Now I feel hungry, what can I have to eat?" Squinkle said to himself. Turning his attention from the wig tree and the mirror bush, he turned round to walk home when he noticed a little tree.... And this one had hamburgers growing all over it!

"Oh Wow! A hamburger tree! Where *are* all these strange plants coming from today?" Squinkle said to himself. Then he heard some giggling and called out "Who's there?" But no-one answered. He didn't stop to think about why there was no answer. Instead he just reached over and plucked one of the burgers from the hamburger tree.

It was delicious.

"Yumm, it's hot." he said, and gobbled it down as fast as he could.

"I think I'll have another one." So he did!

"I'm really thirsty now," he said.

And do you know what? A little way down the road he could see a cola tree, with bottles of cola hanging all over the branches. "It must be my lucky day today, unless someone is playing a trick on me?" he said. Then he hopped and skipped (and burped) his way along to the cola tree. Unfortunately he didn't see the shadowy little shapes wearing sunglasses and watching him from behind the bushes.

Actually it wasn't his lucky day at all. For, as he followed the line of interesting trees and bushes down the road, he was totally unaware that he was being tricked by the Dangerous Potatoes. By following this strange delightful path he was being led deeper and deeper into Bluebell Wood! Squinkle was scoffing a bar of chocolate from a 'bar of chocolate' tree and skipping along quite happily when finally he noticed the bluebells.

"Oh No! Bluebells. I hope this isn't Bluebell Wood," he sniffed.

Then he heard more giggling and cackling and saw the bushes rustling.

"Dangerous Potatoes," he thought as realisation dawned. "This is Bluebell Wood!"

He spluttered on his chocolate.

"But it's day time! I thought Dangerous Potatoes only came out at night?"

Unluckily for him, strange things can happen around Dangerous Potatoes.

Suddenly the sky started to grow dark and the wind started to howl and Squinkle didn't feel quite so safe anymore. Out of nowhere, a total eclipse was forming above him, and he watched in terror as the sun disappeared behind the moon.

"Oh dear. This is kinda like night time," said Squinkle to himself,

The earth beneath his feet started to rumble and move.

# Chapter 3

# Alien Potatoes

Bluebell Wood had been plunged into total darkness by the eclipse and a terrified Squinkle stood aghast as what appeared to be a huge spaceship started to lift up from beneath the ground right in front of him! It was huge. Massive. And sparkly. But most of all unearthly. Squinkle's eyes bulged in fear but he was too terrified to run. Then, as the spaceship hovered ominously in front of him, a door began to open beneath it. A bright blue light shone from inside. Squinkle could see the shape of Dangerous Potatoes with big almond-shaped eyes bouncing toward him through the open door.

"Uh! Oh!" was all he could say. Turning at last to run, he was struck by a blinding flash which froze him to the spot.

"I can't move!" he whimpered helplessly through his teeth. Behind him, the Dangerous Potatoes bounced out of the spaceship and spoke to each other in a strange goggly woggly language.

"Goggly Woggly Goggly Woggly," one said to another, in a bossy voice. But the other got angry and started shouting back.

"GOGGLY WOGGLY GOGGLY WOGGLY!"

The other Potato pulled a huge ray-gun out from nowhere and blew the angry Potato away. ZAPOOOOMMMM.!!!!! The angry Potato exploded into a shower of mash that went all over Squinkle.

Now things took an even stranger turn. Squinkle started to float helplessly toward the spaceship door and the alien Dangerous Potatoes escorted him into a room full of weird equipment and strange noises. Slowly Squinkle was manoeuvered down onto a big table with bright lights over it. The Dangerous Potatoes spoke to each other again.

"Goggly Woggly Goggly Woggly," said one. Another potato got very angry and shouted back ....... " Goggly Woggly Goggly Woggly!" Then the first Dangerous Potato pulled out a ray gun and shot the angry potato, blowing it into a mess of mash.

"What's going on?" whimpered Squinkle, rolling his eyes in panic. "What do you want from me?"

But the potatoes just bounced around the room ignoring Squinkle. Eventually they brought a big metal helmet over to him and fixed it on his head with straps. The helmet had big electrodes and wires coming out of the top of it, which led off to a ginormous television screen. The Dangerous Potatoes started turning knobs and switching switches until the television screen started to flicker on.

"I hope you didn't bring me here to watch television," said Squinkle. "I can do that at home." Then Squinkle watched in dismay as a perfect picture of Wika Waka walking in his training shoes appeared on the screen. "Hey, that's my friend Wika Waka," shouted Squinkle.

All the Dangerous Potatoes turned and watched the screen enviously. A big green square appeared in the top right hand corner of the screen and then zoomed in on the training shoes that went, 'Wika Waka' 'Wika Waka' 'Wika Waka'.

"Coooooooooooooool," said all the Dangerous Potatoes in unison. Some of them were drooling. Then a Dangerous Potato pulled a big lever and a pair of training shoes just like Wika Waka's slowly materialised in a glass box on a table next to Squinkle's head.

"Now that's coooooooool," acknowledged Squinkle in amazement.

# Chapter 4

# Fight! Fight! Fight!

The Dangerous Potatoes all turned to Squinkle and started to talk to each other in goggly woggly language again. “Goggly Woggly Goggly Woggly,” one said. Another got angry and shouted back, “GOGGLY WOGGLY GOGGLY WOGGLY!” And yet another alien potato was blown up by a big ray gun pulled out of nowhere. “CAAASPLOSHHHHHH!” Pieces of potato went everywhere.

“If you keep on like this there won’t be any of you left,” shouted Squinkle angrily.

All the Dangerous Potatoes turned to look at Squinkle then crowded round him. One of them turned a knob and a picture of Squinkle appeared on the television screen. The green box also appeared and then focused in on Squinkle’s mouth, which was talking but made no sound. Then another lever was pulled and a pair of teeth materialised in the glass box on the table just next to Squinkle’s head. “Those look just like my teeth,” said Squinkle. “What would you want those for?”

Then one of the potatoes jumped into the training shoes and put the pair of teeth in his mouth. Instantly he started walking round the room talking in a posh voice. “Oh I say. These shoes are really marvellous darling,” he said.

All the other Dangerous Potatoes started shouting and jumping up and down excitedly.

“GOGGLY WOGGLY GOGGLY WOGGLY,” they shouted.

Squinkle couldn't believe his eyes or his ears. "You must be patient, you can all have a go in a mo, it's my turn first," said the posh potato to the others.

But it was no good! One of them got impatient and shot him with a ray-gun. The posh potato exploded in a shower of mash leaving only the training shoes and pair of teeth lying on the floor. There was chaos as all the potatoes bundled on top of each other in a rush to grab the teeth and shoes. Potato after potato ran around the room wearing the teeth and training shoes until it got blown up by another potato and then the whole performance started over again.

"I wish someone would get me out of here," Squinkle moaned. "If Monkeyman was here she'd know what to do."

Just as he said that Monkeyman appeared on the big television screen. Then amazingly she slowly started to materialize in the glass box on the table next to Squinkle's head. But the Dangerous Potatoes were so busy trying on the training shoes and blowing each other up, they didn't notice. "Monkeyman, how did you get here?" stammered Squinkle in surprise as Monkeyman hurried to untie him.

"I'm not really Monkeyman," said the little girl. "I only look like her. Your brain thought of me and the machine made me. So you see I'm not real at all."

"So how am I going to get out of here?" asked Squinkle.
"Oh, you'll think of something," said the little girl who really really looked like Monkeyman.
"Are you kidding? I'm Squinkle. I'm so silly I could never think of anything clever like that," he said.
"Oh really," said the little girl. "Well you thought of me didn't you?"
"Well yes," replied Squinkle.
"Well then, think of something else useful," she said, and with that she vanished

along with the pair of training shoes and teeth that were keeping the Dangerous Potatoes occupied.

The potatoes all stopped and turned round to see Squinkle standing up. "Oh no, what can I think about that'll get me out of here?" he moaned.

# Chapter 5

# Gravy!

The Dangerous Potatoes were now advancing menacingly towards Squinkle. "What are potatoes scared of?" he wondered, with his eyes squeezed tightly shut. "I know. Gravy!" he shouted.

The potatoes all stopped and looked at each other and repeated, "Gravy?" in unison.

Then they all turned and stared at the glass box where all the other things had come from. Soon it started to rumble and fill up with a dark brown liquid.

"Oh............GRAVY!" they shouted as hundreds of gallons of hot, thick, sticky gravy gushed out of the machine and covered the Dangerous Potatoes. They all turned and bounced and squelched, screaming towards the door.

Squinkle tore off the big metal helmet and threw it to the ground and ran as well.

"Help, let me out!" he wailed.

The spaceship was trying desperately to take off but it couldn't because of the tons of gravy slopping from room to room. Instead it just rolled from side to side tossing the Dangerous Potatoes around like chips in a deep-fat-fryer. Squinkle hammered on the metal door with his fists. "Open up or we're all going to drown in gravy," he shouted. But the door stuck fast. The Potatoes gargled and howled as they sank in the gravy but Squinkle stayed afloat, because at least he could do the doggy-paddle! "I hate gravy," he shouted. "But not as much as I hate Dangerous Potatoes!"

The spaceship was so full of gravy now that it started to stretch like a big squelchy metal balloon. It groaned and heaved until at last it burst wide open, spewing Dangerous Potatoes, pieces of machine and of course Squinkle, into Bluebell Wood. KASPLOSH!!!!!!!! Squinkle rolled under a tree and sat up amongst the bluebells rubbing gravy out of his eyes.

Now with the eclipse long since past, the Dangerous Potatoes weren't only covered in gravy, they had the sunlight in their eyes. They bounced around fizzing and popping like bottles of lemonade. One by one their insides exploded out of the top of their heads just like a fountain, until only saggy empty skins lay on the ground...................dead.

"Wow that was better than firework night," Squinkle said to himself. All the mess (and there was a lot of it) rapidly sank between the bluebells. Quickly forgetting just how much danger he'd been in, Squinkle looked around and said to himself, "It's just like nothing even happened here. I bet if I tried really hard I could pretend it was all a dream." So he did. That was until he got home and his mummy saw him.

"What have you done to your hair and why are you covered in gravy you silly boy?"

Squinkle was so glad to be home he didn't really think about the frightening things he'd seen that day. He was even happy while his mummy told him off.

But that night he had dreams that wouldn't stop. Nightmares that seemed so real, he was too scared to cry out for his mummy. And, in the morning, things got even stranger.........but that's another story.

# The End